The Spooks

The room was a chaos of swirling sheets and deafening noise when, with a wicked smile, Hubert suddenly switched off the television. The room plunged into darkness. Unable to see, the twins tripped over their sheets. Wayne crashed into the sofa where the leggo bag was wrenched from his belt, scattering leggo across the floor. Tracy ran over it and cried out in pain as her bare feet were spiked by its sharp corners. She tripped and fell, sitting hard on the whoopee cushion. As its long moan died away, the light flashed on.

Other titles in the JUGGLERS series:

Elizabeth Lindsay

The Spooks

Illustrated by Jean Baylis

Hippo Books
Scholastic Publications Limited
London

Scholastic Publications Ltd.,
10 Earlham Street, London WC2H 9RX, UK

Scholastic Inc.,
730 Broadway, New York, NY 10003 USA

Scholastic Tab Publications Ltd.,
123 Newkirk Road, Richmond Hill,
Ontario L4C 3G5, Canada

Ashton Scholastic Pty Ltd.,
P O Box 579, Gosford, New South Wales,
Australia

Ashton Scholastic Ltd.,
165 Marua Road, Panmure, Auckland 6,
New Zealand

Published by Scholastic Publications Ltd., 1990

Text copyright © Elizabeth Lindsay
Illustration copyright © Jean Baylis

ISBN 0 590 76390 3

Printed by Cox and Wyman Ltd., Reading, Berks

I
The Grange

The clock struck. One, two, three, four, five, six, seven, eight, nine, ten, eleven, twelve. Or rather it was Ebenezer Spook who struck the clock. The clock had been left long ago by the last inhabitants of the Grange. It no longer wound up or sounded its chimes. Like the house it was decayed and crumbling.

"Bah!" hissed Ebenezer as the big hand of the clock fell to the floor and bounced into a gap between the rotting floorboards. "Bah! Where is everyone? I've struck the witching hour."

A haze, which was Ebenezer, floated upstairs and disappeared through the landing wall. There, in the largest bedroom at the Grange, he found the rest of the Spooks.

"Come on, you Spooks," hissed Ebenezer. "The haunting time is now. The clock has struck."

Dismayed moaning filled the air. Virginia Spook rose up and sank down again.

"Up I say, up!" ordered Ebenezer, reaching out wispy fingers. More moaning followed this command. "What is the matter with you all?" he asked. "In the good old days, the clock struck the witching hour and every last one of us was up and ready to haunt. I've never known such a lazy bunch of Spooks. What's wrong with you?"

"Boredom," sighed Virginia, managing to rise up at last. "It's all very well haunting but we're just going through the motions now no one lives here any more."

"It's no fun if there's no one to scare," said Mary Spook.

"No fun at all," agreed Hubert, the youngest Spook of them all.

"But that's not the point," spluttered Ebenezer. "We're Spooks, and Spooks haunt. Having no one to scare should make no difference at all."

"Well, it does," wailed Mary.

"It does," agreed Virginia.

"It certainly does," said Hubert, shimmering with indignation. "It would be fun to give some person, any person, a great big scare."

"If you won't haunt with me then I must haunt alone," said Ebenezer, turning to go. Virginia shook out her long, ghostly tresses. With a shamefaced look she said, "We'll all come. Of course we must haunt." She beckoned to Hubert and Mary. They followed and one by one vanished through the bedroom wall.

From the witching hour until the crack of dawn the house was alive with creaks and groans, footsteps and doorslams made by invisible, and sometimes faintly visible, moon-lit figures gliding hurriedly by hither and thither. With the first light of morning a silence fell upon the Grange and from that moment, as the sun rose in the sky, nothing disturbed its unkempt yet ancient grandeur.

Nothing disturbed it, that is, until a lorry drew up outside the broken iron gates at the end of the drive. Two men climbed from the lorry and took out a large post and a board with writing on it. They began to hammer. The blows shattered the morning quiet and summoned Hubert Spook to find out what all the noise was about. The men could not see Hubert, but being a Spook, Hubert gave the air a certain chill.

"Cor," said one of the men to his companion. "It's turned a bit blooming nippy." He rubbed the goose pimples on his arms.

"I don't like it here a bit," replied the other.

"I'm glad we don't have to go near the house. This place gives me the creeps."

Hubert ignored the men and tried his best to read the writing on the large board. The first bit was easy: "For Sale". He had trouble with "Hugglet and Evans Estate Agents", and his eye returned to the first words, "For Sale".

"The Grange is for sale," he gasped, the meaning of the words, suddenly striking him.

"I wouldn't buy a dump like this, would you George?" said one of the men. "It'd cost a bit to get it in reasonable condition. It's been let go."

The other man, still rubbing his arms, replied, "Hardly worth the bother, I should think."

Hubert didn't wait to hear any more. He shot back into the house as fast as he could.

"That's strange," said the man. "I've warmed up again, all of a sudden."

"The sun's come out," said his partner.

"The sun was *always* out. A bit odd that." It was, for his goose pimples had gone and he was as warm as toast.

As the men drove off in their lorry it became chilly again by the Grange's iron gates, as Hubert assembled the Spooks there. They gazed at the "For Sale" sign.

"He's right," whispered Ebenezer. "The Grange is for sale. We must be alert and on our guard. We must await events."

"What sort of events?" asked Hubert. Ebenezer didn't know.

10

"Who will buy the house?" said Mary.

"If only we knew," said Virginia, sweeping past her. "Do as Ebenezer says. Wait and see."

There was nothing for it but to be patient. Ebenezer and Virginia found this easy enough, but Mary and Hubert were filled with curiosity. They became thoroughly irritating with all the questions they asked that couldn't be answered.

It was a relief to the older Spooks when the next day a car drove between the broken iron gates and bumped along the rutted drive to the front door. Mary and Hubert leaned from an upstairs window, desperate for a glimpse of the car's passengers. They saw two gentlemen, a lady and two children get out.

The older gentleman, who was wearing a dark suit, patted stray wisps of grey hair into place. He closed the car door after the lady and, with a large iron key, pointed to the impressive, though worn, front door.

"This way please, Mrs Wishwell, Mr Wishwell," he said.

"Thank you, Mr Hugglet," Mrs Wishwell said. "Tracy, Wayne. Come along now."

The two children reluctantly climbed down from the gnarled wisteria which grew high above the door. Tracy kicked Wayne on the way down. Whether by accident or not, who could tell? Wayne kicked Tracy in return. Mr Wishwell put a stop to the ensuing argument by grabbing each of the children by the ear and holding them apart.

"Ouch, Dad," said Tracy. "That hurts."

"Leggo," said Wayne.

"Let this be a warning," said Mr Wishwell. "I want good behaviour, polite behaviour, absolutely none of your nonsense, or you both go back to the car." He let go of the ears. Wayne rubbed his and looked pained. Tracy put her nose in the air and narrowed her eyes. Mr Wishwell looked sternly at them both.

By this time Mr Hugglet had inserted the iron key into the keyhole and was trying to turn it. Mr Wishwell offered his assistance and the two men struggled with the key, Mr Hugglet apologizing all the while. The key would not turn, for the lock was old and rusty and had not been unlocked for years. Mrs Wishwell stood by, smiling and patient, while her terrible offspring grew bored. At last, when Mr Hugglet was about to give up, the key turned, grating metal on metal, and the lock opened with a clunk.

"Welcome to the Grange," cried Mr Hugglet, triumphant but ruffled. He patted more strands of hair into place as the door creaked open. "Pray, follow me." Wayne and Tracy put their hands together and raised their eyes to the heavens. Mr Hugglet, ignoring them, took two steps inside. On the third there was a crunch and his foot disappeared through a rotten floorboard. He sat down with a bump.

"Oh, my goodness," he said. "Do take care.

Perhaps you would be so kind?" He held up a hand to Mr Wishwell. Tracy and Wayne grinned and Mr Wishwell pulled.

"The Grange is a little more decayed than I thought," he said, when upright.

"It's cold in here," said Mrs Wishwell. She shivered as Hubert Spook glided past her shoulder.

"Just in need of a bit of an airing," smiled Mr Hugglet. "Follow me, please, to the dining room."

"Come along, twins," said Mrs Wishwell.

"Twins!" repeated Hubert. "Gosh, twins!" Although, of course, no one heard him except Mary.

"Real twins!" said Mary, joining Hubert as he followed the Wishwells to the dining room.

"This is a very pleasant room," said Mr Hugglet, pushing wide the door. "With a delightful view of the garden." There was a sharp crack and the door leaned over at an odd angle. The twins laughed loudly.

"Do all the doors do that?" giggled Tracy.

"Can we have a go?" howled Wayne.

Mr Hugglet went red, whether from

embarrassment or anger it was hard to tell. He ignored the twins.

"Of course, you do understand that much work needs to be done in order restore the Grange to its former glory. Unfortunately, it has been badly neglected over the years."

"Such a shame," said Mrs Wishwell. "It's in such a beautiful spot and I do so like the garden. Plenty of space for the children to play in. Show me the kitchen, please, Mr Hugglet."

"Of course, dear lady, follow me."

Mr Hugglet stepped across the hallway as if walking on stepping stones. The kitchen was at the back of the house and, relieved there had been no more mishaps, he led the way in. Mrs Wishwell let out a gasp of dismay.

"It smells!" she groaned. "It smells disgusting."

"Just a little bit of damp and dry rot, I'm afraid," said Mr Hugglet. "But it has enormous potential."

"Oh, dear," said Mr Wishwell. "It is a bit of a mess."

Tracy saw an opportunity for escape.

"Quick, upstairs," she whispered to Wayne.

Before anyone noticed the two of them ran for it.

"Great banisters," said Tracy at the top.

"Yeah," said Wayne. "What for?"

"Sliding down, stupid."

"Don't call me stupid," said Wayne, biffing his sister.

The pair of them ran along the landing and pushed open the end door.

"Cor," said Wayne. "The bathroom."

"Look at the bath. It's on legs," said Tracy. The two of them jumped into it.

"It's brilliant," they cried. They balanced on the side of the bath clinging to one another.

"When I say jump, we jump," said Tracy.

"JUMP!" They landed in the middle of the bathroom floor. The bath sagged.

"Cor, look at that," said Wayne. The legs of the bath were lost from view. From underneath them came a rending sound. The twins scurried to the safety of the landing. Something huge fell with a crash to the floor below. There were yells of outrage and dust swirled upwards from between the bathroom floorboards.

Tracy and Wayne hurried to the top of the stairs, jumped astride the banister and slid down. Whoosh. Whoosh. One after the other.

"Great," said Wayne.

"Yeah, great," said Tracy.

Dust billowed from the kitchen door. Mr and Mrs Wishwell stood busily dusting down Mr Hugglet whose suit had undergone a colour change from dark to light.

"What were you doing?" asked Mr Wishwell.

"Nothing," said Tracy.

"Honest, Dad," said Wayne.

"Well, something must have caused the kitchen ceiling to cave in."

"It wasn't us, Dad. It really wasn't," they chorused.

"Do you know, I think we should buy the Grange," said Mrs Wishwell.

"Dear lady," gasped Mr Hugglet. "A wise decision."

"And pull it down."

"Pull it down!" Hubert Spook was stunned.

"She wants to pull it down!" Mary Spook was wide-eyed.

"Yes, and build a nice modern house. It'd be draught-free and much more comfortable than this. We'd have this lovely spot, a nice garden and a wonderful new house as well."

"It's certainly something to think about," said Mr Wishwell.

"I like it as an old house," said Tracy.

"So do I," said Wayne.

"Quiet," said Mr Wishwell.

"Yes, well, it's certainly an idea," said Mr Hugglet. "Let me drive you back to my office and we can discuss the matter further."

Mary and Hubert didn't wait to hear more.

"They want to what?" said Ebenezer, thunderstruck.

"Pull it down."

"Pull the Grange down? But they can't," whispered Virginia. "This is *our* house."

The Spooks listened as the front door banged. They heard the car doors slam and the engine start.

"Yes," hissed Ebenezer. "This is our house and whatever else happens we won't let them pull it down! We'll fight to save the Grange. That's what we'll do, now and forever more!"

The Spooks glided to the nearest window and watched as the car carried Mr Hugglet and the Wishwells down the drive and out of sight.

2
The Demolition

From the day the Wishwells visited the Grange a watch was kept by the Spooks. There was always one of them near the gate. Nothing happened for nearly two weeks, except that the Grange was thoroughly haunted every night and during the day as well. Not a single Spook moaned, except when haunting, and no one complained of being bored.

It was two weeks to the day when the lorry returned. Virginia was sitting upon one of the tall stone gateposts, running wispy fingers through her ghostly tresses as she watched. It took the two men no time at all to hammer a sign onto the "For Sale" board. It read "SOLD".

"Can't think who'd want to buy it," said one of the men.

"More money than sense, I reckon," rep-

lied his workmate. With that the men drove off. Virginia slid to the ground and made her way indoors.

"I think we can assume the Wishwells are the purchasers as no one else has been to see the Grange," hissed Ebenezer, when he heard the news. "We must be alert, my fellow Spooks, alert to the danger we are in."

Virginia went back to her position on the gatepost. Hubert perched nearby on the broken gate.

"What's going to happen?" he asked.

"If only we knew," said Virginia. "The Grange has never been sold before."

"Whatever happens we mustn't let them pull it down," said Hubert. "We mustn't."

"We shan't," said Virginia. "We shall stop them by hook or by crook."

Suddenly, a distant chugging could be heard, and something tall and yellow appeared above the line of trees at the roadside.

"Fetch the others, Hubert," ordered Virginia, standing on her gatepost to get a better view. Hubert didn't wait to be asked twice. He sped to the house.

"What exactly is it?" Virginia wondered. The machine crept closer and closer. Virginia noted its caterpillar tracks, the tall crane at the front and, nestling between the caterpillar tracks below the driver's cab, a large iron ball. She had never seen a machine like it.

The other Spooks joined her and stood on the gate.

"It's a war machine," said Ebenezer. "I think."

"What will it do?" asked Virginia.

"I can't tell," hissed Ebenezer, "but we must be ready to take evasive action should it stop here."

Stop there it did. Right outside the gates of the Grange. The man in the cab switched off the engine and the Spooks watched as he climbed from his cab and paced the distance between the gateposts.

"Should go through all right," he mumbled to himself. "Better wait for Sid just in case."

The man leaned on a caterpillar track and picked his teeth with a fingernail. The Spooks waited on the gateposts anxiously.

Sid arrived on a motorbike. He roared up the road and stopped with a skid by the war machine.

"Where've you been?" grumbled the waiting driver.

"Sorry, Pete," said Sid. "I got lost. But I'm here now so it's all right."

"Is it?" said Pete irritably. "Park the bike. Make it snappy and see me through this gate."

"Keep your hair on," said Sid, but he did as he was told. Peter got into the cab and started the engine. Black smoke rose from the exhaust. He swung the machine round and pointed it at the gate.

"It's going to be a tight squeeze," shouted Sid, and beckoned the machine forward. Slowly the tracks edged their way towards the gateposts. With barely an inch to spare on either side the machine passed through and rumbled up the drive, the crane bending a branch of the old chestnut tree until it snapped. The branch hung shattered and limp.

"Retreat to the house," ordered Virginia. Ebenezer was speechless with rage. He loved the chestnut tree.

"Clumsy oaf," he hissed. They had to drag him to the house. "My lovely tree," he

24

wailed. "Planted when I was a snippling, a wee lad like one of them."

"Ebenezer, that's enough," said Virginia. "We've work to do. We've got to learn to work the war machine for ourselves."

"What?" said Ebenezer. "Work that!"

"That's what I said. We must overrule their commands. When they tell it to do one thing we'll tell it to do another."

"I get it," said Hubert. "I'll go and be with the driver. I'll learn what to do."

"I'll come with you," said Mary. They were soon in the driver's cab looking over Pete's shoulder.

The engine was ticking over and Pete was having a pick at his teeth. It was Sid who was busy. He was sorting out the chain and tightening some nuts with a large spanner. The chain now had the giant iron ball on the end of it.

"Take it away," he called to Pete, waving the spanner above his head. Pete pulled a lever and the slack in the chain was taken up. Slowly the ball was lifted from its resting place and began to swing from the tall yellow crane. Mary and Hubert watched every move of every lever and saw the effect each had on the ball. The crane lifted the giant ball up high until it swung menacingly above the roof. Pete leaned out of the cab and shouted, "I'll start at the front."

"Might as well," said Sid.

"I don't know why, but it's like a fridge in the cab, and I've got the heater on," shouted Pete. Sid shrugged. The sun was streaming down and the engine was hot. He thought it impossible Pete should be cold, but he didn't say anything; he knew Pete was already in a bad mood.

Slowly the ball swung away from the house and back again. It came in close to the front wall as if to hit it, which is what Pete and Sid – and Ebenezer and Virginia, watching from the house – expected it to do. It didn't. The ball swung past the wall and out across the garden. Sid looked up at the cab. Pete was pulling hard at a lever which seemed stuck. He didn't know that Hubert and Mary were pulling it the other way. Suddenly they let go. Pete nearly fell over as the lever shot towards him. The ball swung round so fast, the weight of it lifted one caterpillar track from the ground. For a moment it looked as if the machine would topple over. Sid was astonished.

"What's up?" he shouted.

"Lever got stuck," Pete shouted back. "It's never done that before."

"Better be careful then."

"I will. Don't you worry," shouted Pete. Mary and Hubert were victorious.

"Don't you see?" said Mary. "We need to keep the ball going backwards and forwards in bigger and bigger swings."

"You're right," grinned Hubert. "Are you ready?"

Levers were pulled and knobs turned. Pete became very confused. The ball swung this way, the ball swung that way, but never did it get anywhere near the walls of the house. The cab began to turn with the swing of the ball. Pete fought the controls. It was a losing battle. He couldn't see the Spooks, so he never knew which lever was going to move next. Suddenly the cab swung back on

itself. Sid ran for cover. Pete put his hands over his head and ducked. The chain whipped against the cab and wound itself around it. The crane buckled; the cab windows shattered. Pete switched off the engine.

The Spooks were beside themselves with joy. The war machine was broken. Seething with rage, Pete clambered from his cab and surveyed the damage.

"Never, never in all my days have I known anything like it," he spluttered. "Ruined. It's ruined."

Sid crept from his place of safety but stayed well back.

"They'll have to pay for it," said Pete. "They will. I've never known anything like it. Some unseen power took control."

"Unseen power!" said Sid.

"That's what I said. Hands other than mine were working those controls, Sid."

Sid went white. "You mean, like, haunting it?"

"You know me, I'm a good crane operator. Under normal working conditions I could demolish this dump in a day. But the conditions aren't normal. It's freezing in that cab, and it was a battle trying to move them controls."

"Freezing!" whispered Sid, still the same pallid shade. "Not you moving the controls!"

"So let's go," said Pete.

"Yes, let's," said Sid. He could hardly wait.

Mary and Hubert hovered in the driver's cab until the damaged war machine had been seen off the premises. The Spooks watched from the gate as it chugged forlornly away.

"Victory!" cried Hubert.

"We won!" cried Mary.

Virginia and Ebenezer didn't cheer.

"True," said Ebenezer, "the first victory is ours, but what is to come?"

Yes, what was to come? The Spooks had to think of that.

3
Modernization

Peace reigned at the Grange for four days. The caterpillar tracks made by the war machine were washed away by a heavy fall of rain, making everything seem as usual. But things were not as usual. The estate agents "SOLD" sign hanging at the gate reminded them of it. So the Spooks were quick to gather when an emerald green car turned into the drive on the morning of the fifth day.

The car halted in front of the house and Mr and Mrs Wishwell climbed from the front, the twins from the back.

"It's just as well that man Pete was such a nincompoop," said Mr Wishwell, "or the Grange would be a pile of rubble."

"It's lucky we found out," said Mrs Wishwell. She didn't look pleased. What had the Wishwells found out? The Spooks were desperate to know.

"I like the old house best," said Tracy, leaping onto the wisteria.

"Get off that tree at once," said Mr Wish-well. He struggled to unlock the front door.

"You two children can play in the garden, while your mother and I decide what needs to be done."

"Why can't we help decide?" asked Wayne.

"Because you can't. Go and play outside."

"Right," said Mrs Wishwell. "If the regulations won't allow us to knock the house down and build a new one, we must make this one as modern as we can. I'm going to make a list of things to be done." She took a notebook from her handbag and went into the house. Mr Wishwell followed.

"Not allowed to knock the house down," Ebenezer sighed. "What a relief!" The Spooks went dancing from room to room, causing dust to rise and Mrs Wishwell to complain of the filth.

"It'll get worse before it gets better," said Mr Wishwell, thinking of the mess the builders would make. "But it'll make us a very nice house."

A door slammed above them and the floorboards creaked.

"I told the twins," said Mr Wishwell. "I wish for once they would listen."

"They won't do any harm," said Mrs Wishwell. "Shall we start in the kitchen?"

The noise hadn't been made by the twins. It had been made by the Spooks, but the Wishwells didn't notice anything strange.

Not even when they got so chilly their arms became covered in goose pimples.

"Central heating will be a big improvement," said Mrs Wishwell as they left the house. "Come along, twins."

The twins appeared from round the side of the house. Wayne had fallen from the hayloft and cut his knee. A handkerchief was tied round the wound and he was limping, with an arm around Tracy's shoulder for support.

"Oh, now what's he done?" said Mrs Wishwell. She bundled Wayne into the back of the car.

"Home as fast as we can before the germs get to that knee," she cried.

Mr Wishwell drove so fast down the driveway that his passengers almost bounced to the roof. The Spooks watched them go with glee. The Grange was safe. Safe from demolition. True, it was going to be modernized . . . .

"I wonder what that will mean?" said Ebenezer. "We shall have to wait and see." The house was safe, though, and that was more important than anything else.

It was when the workmen arrived that the Spooks began to understand what a turmoil making the house modern was going to mean. They were astonished at the amount of things that needed to be changed.

When all the plaster had been knocked from the walls, all the ceilings taken down and many joists removed, the Spooks became indignant. The inside of the Grange was unrecognizable. If you stood in the cellar you could see the roof, and when the workman took off the old tiles you could see the sky. The Wishwells were pleased by the destruction and called it progress. The Spooks saw it as another kind of demolition and rallied round for a save-the-walls campaign. But the workmen didn't knock the walls down. Instead, large machines arrived and what was left of the house was sprayed with a foul-smelling chemical which reached all the nooks and crannies, places that hadn't been uncovered in years.

"Very good," said Mr Wishwell, beaming and holding his nose. "That'll put a stop to the rot."

"Very good!" said Virginia. "The man's a lunatic. What's good about this?" Her ghostly tresses swung wildly. With an angry wave of her hand she surveyed the damage. "I think it's disgusting. There's nowhere to go that hasn't got holes in it, including the attic where you can see the sky."

"Yes, yes," said Ebenezer. "But, you see, the old rotten bits have got to go before the new bits can replace them. The Grange was more rotten than we thought. In the end it would have fallen down."

"Goodness," said Hubert.

"Goodness, indeed, Master Hubert," said Ebenezer.

"That makes it much better this way," said Mary.

"I think so, Mistress Mary," nodded Ebenezer. "I think so."

"I hope you're right, Ebenezer," said Virginia. "It seems to me everything is just spoilt."

"Well, we'll just have to wait and see," Ebenezer replied.

"That's what you always say and I'm fed

up with hearing it." Virginia swept into the garden, causing a whirlwind of dust which smothered Mr Wishwell and made him sneeze.

The workmen began to dig a long trench which went from the front door, along the drive, to the road. Cables and pipes were laid in it. New joists and rafters were put in and the roof was covered with new slates. Ebenezer nodded his satisfaction. The Grange really was being cared for. The trench along the drive was filled in, wires were run up the walls and underneath the joists, new ceilings were erected, new floor-boards were nailed to the floors. The walls and ceilings were plastered with fresh, pink plaster. Radiators were fixed to the walls and light bulbs hung from the ceilings.

The Spooks were fascinated by the lights. They saw the electrician test them, switching them on and off. The hall light could be switched on from the landing and the land-ing light from the hall. The Spooks simply had to try them. They played with the lights until the electrician became confused and

angry. In the end Virginia said they must
stop.

"We mustn't give the Wishwells an excuse

for not moving in," she said. "I was wrong. I'm glad the house has been modernized. It feels like a proper home, like it did when I was a girl, long before I became a Spook. I'm glad it's going to be lived in again."

Broken windowpanes were replaced and the windows painted. Wallpaper was hung, the old oak staircase and banisters were polished. A large lorry brought carpets and the floorboards were covered with soft new pile in a variety of colours.

The gloomy kitchen was transformed into Mrs Wishwell's dream. There was a shiny sink, a large electric cooker, a dishwasher, a refrigerator, a freezer and a microwave. Gleaming worktops stretched around the walls. The Spooks had never seen anything like it and wondered what it was all for.

The bathroom too underwent a transformation. The pink bathroom suite and tiles and luxury thick-pile pink carpet gave it a new and fresh atmosphere. Gone were the old cast-iron bath with legs and the cranky iron cistern.

The garden was not left out of this transformation. The collapsed conservatory was rebuilt with double-glazed panes, the lawn was cut, the flowerbeds were weeded. The rutted drive was made smooth with a covering of tarmac. The gateposts were repaired and the broken gates mended and rehung. Last, but not least, the "SOLD" sign was taken down.

The Grange had been given a face-lift. It gleamed in the autumn sunlight. The chestnut trees shed a leaf or two and the Spooks danced among them as they fluttered to the earth. Gone were the workmen, leaving a job well done. All was ready for the Wishwells to move in. The Grange and the Spooks waited for them.

4
Moving In

The huge lorry edged its way between the gateposts and brushed the chestnut tree. The branches beat like drumsticks against the words "Bodge and Ridgeworth Removals", scratching the paint. The Wishwells" green car followed the lorry. Both drew up outside the front door of the Grange. Four men jumped from the lorry; the Wishwells tumbled from the car. It was moving-in day.

Mr Wishwell greeted the men and unlocked the front door. Mrs Wishwell opened the boot of the car and took out a large cardboard box.

"I expect you could all do with a nice cup of tea," she said. The men nodded appreciatively. Yes, they could. They'd worked hard loading the lorry. The Wishwells had an awful lot of furniture and some of it was very heavy.

Mrs Wishwell carried the box into the hall, across the new purple carpet to the kitchen, where the shiny, blue worktops and glossy, red and beige floor gleamed a welcome to her.

Virginia Spook followed Mrs Wishwell into the kitchen. She was curious to know how tea would be made now that the old kitchen range had gone. Not that she herself had ever made the tea when she was alive. It had been prepared by the cook or the scullery maid. But she remembered how it used to be done. She had watched often enough. Mrs Wishwell filled the electric kettle at the sink and plugged it in. Virginia observed the kettle with some interest and saw that when it came to the boil it switched itself off.

"Very modern indeed," was her verdict, as she glided into the hall to tell the others. Ebenezer, Mary and Hubert were draped over the landing banisters, watching intently as the men carried tea chest after tea chest into the hall.

Mr Wishwell, who had followed his wife into the kitchen, returned with a tray and

began handing round mugs of tea and offering biscuits. The men leaned on the tea chests and did their best not to drop crumbs.

"Twins," called Mrs Wishwell in a high voice. "Twins."

The twins, who had not so far put in an appearance inside the Grange, called, "Yes, Mum."

Their mother looked around, trying to locate the sound of their voices. The twins' faces were in line with the Spooks on the landing. They could see them looking in from the window high above the front door.

"Yes, Mum!" the twins called again, grinning.

Mrs Wishwell looked up and gasped. Mr Wishwell followed her shocked gaze. He went outside and found Tracy and Wayne high in the wisteria.

"Come down at once," he bellowed. "If I've told you once, I've told you a hundred times! You are *not* to climb the wisteria."

"Oh, dear," said Mrs Wishwell. "We'll have to cut it down. It's the only way to stop them." The Spooks rose up in a fury.

"Cut down the wisteria!" hissed Ebenezer.

"Never," cried Virginia.

Climbing down was much more difficult for the twins than climbing up had been. The Spooks saw to that. There were prickles everywhere which hadn't been there before and branches sprang and slapped them with a sharp sting that was quite unexpected. By the time they reached the ground they had already decided never to climb the wisteria again. Their legs and arms were red and sore. They rubbed them, feeling sorry for themselves.

"That'll teach you to do as you're told," said their unsympathetic father.

"Oh, dear," said their mother when she saw them and wondered where the First Aid box was.

Mr Wishwell went to the car and took out two bats and a ball. He handed them to the twins, who took them sulkily.

"Right," said Mr Wishwell. "Off you go and play on the lawn. When we get your things into your rooms we'll call you."

"Why've we got to go and play?" said Tracy.

"We'll work quicker if you're not falling about under our feet," said Mr Wishwell. "You'll have plenty of sorting out to do later. Make the most of your opportunity."

Wayne scuffed at the ground. He was thinking they could climb into the hayloft again, even though it had been declared out of bounds since that cut knee incident.

"Come on, Tracy, let's go," he said. He waved his bat and appeared to make obedi-

ently for the lawn. Tracy followed him reluctantly. As they went he whispered something in her ear. She nodded. The two began to bat the ball backwards and forwards to each other for as long as Mr Wishwell watched. As soon as he turned away the bats were dumped on the grass and the twins ran off. Mr Wishwell was too busy directing the removal men to notice.

Panting, the twins arrived in the stableyard at the back of the Grange. So far this set of buildings had remained unmodernized while the Wishwells decided what to do with them. They were full of old bits of

farm machinery. The door to the hayloft creaked on its rusty hinges as Wayne pulled it open. He and Tracy slipped through into the dim stables, where their noses smelt must and mildew. The place was thick with cobwebs. It had lain untouched for years. In the far corner was a set of wooden steps which led up to the loft. It was on these steps that Wayne had tripped.

"Watch where you're treading," said Tracy, blinking as her eyes accustomed themselves to the gloom.

"I am," said Wayne.

There was a sudden chill draught which set the cobwebs swaying and lifted wisps of old straw and hay. The twins shivered, but didn't notice Hubert glide up the steps ahead of them. Mary followed behind them. When the twins got to the loft they were very chilly.

"It was warm up here last time, wasn't it?" said Wayne.

"Well, it's flippin' cold now," said Tracy. "I wonder why?"

The hayloft was draped with heavy cobwebs carrying the dust of years. The twins did their best to avoid them, and made their way to the middle of the loft.

"Wayne! Wayne! Look at this," cried Tracy. She took hold of an old iron ring in the floor. "It's a trap door."

"They mustn't pull the ring. The floor's not safe," said Mary, seeing at once what the twins were oblivous of.

"They never do as they're told, these two," said Hubert.

"And you always do, I suppose," grinned Mary.

Tracy pulled on the ring, leaving Hubert no time to reply. Wayne helped Tracy pull.

"Quick," said Hubert. "Knock them back with cobwebs, the silly idiots."

As fast as they could the Spooks threw cobwebs into the twins' faces. The shock and surprise of this sudden attack had the desired effect. The twins let go of the ring and toppled backwards. They pulled at the cobweb blankets glued to their faces, spitting and gasping for breath. The floor where they had stood but a moment before crumbled away, leaving a gaping hole.

"Cor," said Wayne.

"Heck," said Tracy. "We were standing there."

"We were lucky the wind blew when it did," said Wayne. "These cobwebs saved us."

"Better scarper," said Tracy, and they scuttled back down the wooden steps and ran outside.

Wayne burst into fits of laughter when he took a look at Tracy.

"I don't know what you're laughing at," said Tracy. "You look like you've come out of the chamber of horrors." They were both filthy. Their heads, faces, clothes and hands were covered in a thick grime.

"Quick," said Tracy. "We'd better get back." They ran to the lawn and picked up their bats. Bit bat, bit bat went the ball on the bats. At first Mrs Wishwell smiled when she saw them. Then she yelled.

When the lorry finally drove away, Mr and Mrs Wishwell each gave a huge sigh of relief. The twins were confined to their bedrooms and Mr Wishwell, helped by Mrs Wishwell, and watched curiously by all the Spooks, began to put the twins' filthy clothes into the front-loader washing machine.

"A washing machine, eh?" said Ebenezer. He remembered washing being done in the old copper boiler in the outhouse. It had been hard work for the laundry maid, who had spent all day up to her armpits in soap suds.

Mr Wishwell filled the washing powder dispenser and Mrs Wishwell selected the programme. She read the instruction booklet carefully.

"Programme B," she said. "Heavily soiled with pre-wash. What a lot of bother those twins cause." She switched the machine on. "Egg, oven chips and beans for tea," she said, as the water swished and the clothes began to turn, leaving the Spooks spellbound.

Appliances clicked and whirred. Mr Wishwell went upstairs to escort his dirty children to the bathroom, while Mrs Wishwell took the chips from the freezer.

"Modernization," hissed Ebenezer in wonder.

It was true that the Spooks were disappointed by the Wishwell's choice of decor. They decided that the best they could call the colour schemes was lurid.

"Whoever would have chosen that green and put it with that purple but them," Virginia, said surveying the hall. In her day it had been painted a discreet off-white, which had toned delightfully with the old oak floor.

"Yuk, yuk," sid Mary.

"It is a little loud," agreed Ebenezer.

"We just have to face it," said Virginia. "They have absolutely no taste at all."

"Don't be a snob, Virginia," said Hubert. "They're great when it comes to machines."

"How dare you call me a snob, Hubert," said Virginia, flaring up.

"Now, now, one and all," said Ebenezer. "Let's go back to the kitchen and see how the washing's doing."

"Very well," said Virginia. "I'm going to experiment with the electric kettle on my own." She glared at Hubert. Hubert glared back, then grinned. It was so easy to get Virginia riled.

"Don't be a meany, Hubert," said Mary.

The Wishwells' first day at the Grange came to an end and by ten o'clock they were all in bed, sleeping the sleep of the exhausted which falls on those moving house. Slowly the moon crept across the sky, marking the stillness of the night with its white glow. The house slumbered.

There was a creak on the stair and a shadow crossed a moonbeam which fell on the hall floor. It was Ebenezer Spook looking for a clock. The digital one in the kitchen he didn't even recognize as a clock. "24.00" meant nothing to him. There was a clock in the living room which looked like a clock but didn't have a tick. Would it chime at midnight, he wondered? To be on the safe side he fetched the discarded baked bean tin from the rubbish bin and a fork from the sink. These articles glided through the air, as if transporting themselves to the living room. He waited. The little hand faced the twelve and the big hand crept up to join it. There was not a hint of a chime.

"Bah," wheezed Ebenezer, and struck the empty tin. One, two, three, four, five, six, seven, eight, nine, ten, eleven, twelve. The witching hour. The hour of the full moon. The Spooks had been looking forward to it. The house stirred, suddenly full of shadows.

5
The Hauntings Begin

Clouds drew across the night sky and covered the moon, blotting out its light. The Grange was plunged into sudden blackness. The wind which drove the clouds moaned about the walls of the old house. The curtains shivered. Ebenezer, a mere wisp in the blackness, chuckled. "Let the hauntings begin." His chuckle was taken up by the other Spooks, until chuckles echoed through the house. The Wishwells slept on, oblivious. It was the deep, untroubled sleep of the very tired.

"Onward Spooks," cried Ebenezer in a harsh whisper. "We'll give them a night to remember, these Wishwells."

The moon made a brief appearance, sending beams across the hall carpet as Ebenezer let out a long, low wail, enough to set a chill in the hearts of all who heard it. Four shadows melted across the hallway. Hubert to swing on the living room door, Virginia to the kitchen, whilst Ebenezer, followed by Mary, glided upstairs.

Hubert leapt at the living room door, which had been left ajar. It swung open. Hubert swung the door closed again, then swung it open. The swinging became more and more violent as Hubert became more and more frustrated.

"It doesn't creak. It hasn't a single groan any more," he cried. "They've oiled it." There was a terrific bang as he slammed the door shut in disgust. Mr Wishwell grunted in his sleep. Mrs Wishwell scratched her nose and turned over. Tracy and Wayne slept on undisturbed.

It was Ebenezer who nearly jumped out of his skin.

"What was that?" he asked, spinning round. Mary clung to Ebenezer and said, "I think it was Hubert."

"Well, if it was, go and tell him not to do it again and to get creaking at once."

Obediently Mary went downstairs. She

found Hubert sitting on the bottom step sobbing.

"My door's ruined. They've oiled it. It doesn't creak and groan any more," he said.

"Oh, dear," said Mary. She put her arms around Hubert. "I've just had a horrible thought."

"What?" asked Hubert, swallowing his tears.

"Well," said Mary, giving herself a moment to think things through. "Everything's new, isn't it? New floorboards, new ceilings, oiled door hinges, that kind of thing. I don't think we're going to be able to creak and groan in the same way we did before."

"Why not?"

"Because all the new things don't have creaks and groans. That's why not."

"You could be right." Hubert thought for a moment. "If that's true, how are we going to do our hauntings?" he asked.

"I think it's going to be a bit of problem," said Mary. "We're going to have to think of new things to do."

Upstairs Ebenezer was beginning to come to the same conclusion. He paced the landing as he had always done, ever since he could remember. The effect until now had been the most satisfying splinter-crackling of floorboards. Now there was nothing, not a sound, for the floorboards were new and covered in carpet. If they had even the slightest creak it was muffled by the thick yellow pile.

"Bah!" said Ebenezer. "Bah!" He nipped through the wall into Mr and Mrs Wishwell's bedroom. Mr Wishwell turned on to his back and began to snore in long, loud, sonorous waves, with lip-smacking out-breaths and long, rattling in-breaths which made the loudest snores Ebenezer had ever heard. He looked expectantly at Mrs Wishwell, thinking she must wake at any moment, the noise was so loud. But she lay lost in slumber, a faint smile playing on her lips, quite undisturbed by her snoring husband.

Ebenezer patted her hand, impressed. In a moment Mrs Wishwell was awake. She screamed. The noise was sudden and unexpected. Ebenezer quickly melted from the room and joined Mary and Hubert at the bottom of the stairs.

"There, there, dear," said Mr Wishwell, roused momentarily from his sleep. "Just a bad dream." He put his arm about her and was asleep again in a trice. Mrs Wishwell switched on the bedroom light. She looked at her hand, which was quite as it had always been. She looked around the bedroom, which was also unchanged.

"Yes," she sighed. "A bad dream, except I could've sworn something touched my hand. Something cold like a dead fish." She shivered, took a last look round the room, switched off the light and snuggled into the crook of Mr Wishwell's arm. She was soon lost in the peaceful slumber from which Ebenezer had disturbed her.

Downstairs in the kitchen, Virginia wasn't having much success either. Her favourite haunting had been to turn on the cold water tap over the old stone sink. At one time she would have had all the pipes in the house rattling and clanking and thudding and banging as if they would knock the house down any second. But the shiny chrome taps in the new stainless-steel sink turned on and off with such ease. Try as she might, Virginia could not get a single pipe clunk from either of them.

Another haunting she had used to great effect was to open the air vent on the old kitchen range so that when the wind blew it moaned down the chimney in a most gratifying and ghostly manner. Virginia turned from the taps in disgust and surveyed the shining electric cooker. The old kitchen range had gone, but perhaps the new range, as she thought of the cooker, might manage the same trick.

It took Virginia some moments to realize that nothing happened when she opened the oven door except that the light came on. This new range may have been standing in the chimney breast where the old one had once stood but clearly it was not connected to the chimney. It worked in an altogether different way. To get it hot for cooking it had to be switched on in the same way a switch was flicked to turn on the electric lights. It was wires that made it work, not burning wood and coal. Although Virginia was disappointed that her favourite hauntings were impossible, she was, nevertheless, intrigued by the oven. She went into the hall to look for Ebenezer, and found him with the others at the bottom of the stairs.

"It's not going to be quite as easy as I thought," said Ebenezer. "All this modernization has put a damper on our old hauntings. Things don't work like they did."

"That's just what I've been finding," said Virginia. "I can't get so much as a peep from the pipes."

"Nor I a creak from the floorboards," said Ebenezer.

"Nor I a squeak from the door," muttered Hubert.

"I didn't even try to clank the cistern in the bathroom," said Mary.

"How could you?" said Hubert. "It's not there any more."

"There, you see, I'd forgotten!"

The Spooks sat for a while in silence, pondering the changes the Wishwells had brought to the Grange. It was Virginia who spoke first.

"If we can't haunt with our old hauntings, then we must find some new ones," she said.

"Good idea," said Mary.

"That's what I've been thinking," said Ebenezer.

"But what new ones?" said Hubert. "I can't think of any."

"That's because we've been doing the same old thing for ages and ages," said Virginia. "We must look around and use our imaginations. Let's get to it and meet back here to share our discoveries."

The Spooks departed once again. Hubert glided into the living room; Virginia returned to the kitchen. Ebenezer and Mary went back upstairs.

"Look carefully, with new eyes," whispered Ebenezer to Mary, as she glided into the bathroom. Then he turned his attention to the landing. He switched on the landing light and switched it off again. He preferred the shadowy darkness.

"If only there was something I could rattle, like an old suit of armour," he thought.

Once more Ebenezer glided into the Wishwells' bedroom. Mr Wishwell had turned over and his snoring had stopped. But heavy breathing told Ebenezer the Wishwells were still fast asleep. A box of tissues on the dressing table caught his attention. He took hold of the tissue that was draped half out of the box. With barely a tug it floated into the air and there was the next tissue ready to be pulled. Ebenezer pulled it, and the next, and the next, until the bedroom was littered with tissues. They floated onto the floor and covered the bed. Soon the box was empty.

"That was a good haunting," he thought. "If a little quiet." He looked about him for something that would make a noise. He flapped the curtains hopefully, and was rewarded with a clacking sound. Glancing up, he saw that they hung from round wooden rings that ran along a wooden pole. The click-clacking of the rings was music to his ears. He drew the curtains one way and then the other. The curtains billowed; the rings clacked. It was most satisfactory, except that the noise had no effect at all on the Wishwells. They stayed fast asleep. With one last defiant gesture, Ebenezer flung open the curtains, making the rings clack like a chorus of castanets. Then he melted through the wall and went to find Mary in the bathroom.

Ebenezer tugged at the light switch. A most extraordinary sight met his eyes. The bathroom was covered in long pink festoons. They hung from the mirror, the light, the shower cubicle and the lavatory. The bath was a sea of pink waves. Mary had discovered the toilet rolls and had spent many happy minutes unrolling all twelve of them.

"Isn't it pretty?" she sighed.

"Yes, very," said Ebenezer. He picked up a can of shaving foam and wondered what it did. He pressed the button on top of the can and foam sprayed on to the pink carpet.

"Oh, it's lovely," said Mary. "Let me have a go." She leaned over the bath and gave the pink waves foaming white crests. She laughed as she sprayed and was sad when the tin was suddenly empty.

"Come," said Ebenezer, surveying the bathroom with satisfaction. "Let's find the others."

They found Hubert in the living room sitting in front of a box watching silent pictures that moved. Ebenezer and Mary retreated from the box in surprise. It was the first time any of the Spooks had seen a television.

"Master Hubert, come away," gasped Ebenezer.

"It's all right," said Hubert. "I can make it come and I can make it go. Watch." He pressed the on-off switch and the screen went blank.

"But what is it?" said Ebenezer. "It must be a special kind of picture box."

"It is," said Hubert. "Look, its got wires."

"Ah, wires," said Ebenezer, as if that explained everything. Hubert switched the television back on again. He was enjoying the moving pictures. Curious, Ebenezer turned a button. Voices burst into the room. The three Spooks fled into the hall to the sound of gunfire, the thud of hoof beats and the shouts of men riding across a desert.

"It's haunted," said Ebenezer shakily. "The box is haunted."

"No, that's not it," said Hubert. "I think it's meant to do that." He wriggled across the floor in case the men in the box could see him, and switched the television off.

"See," he said. "If you press they go – and if you press again they come." He switched the television on and adjusted the sound.

"Can I have a go?" said Mary. She pressed once and the television went off. She pressed again and the television came on. Ebenezer followed the wire at the back of the television to the plug in the wall. He pulled out the plug and the television went off.

"How strange," he said. "How very strange."

He was interrupted in his musings by Virginia, who glided into the living room. She tossed her head and her ghostly tresses rippled like seaweed in water.

"Come and see what I've done," she said proudly.

The Spooks followed Virginia to the kitchen, where they were met by the ping of the microwave, the swish of the washing machine and the whirr of the fan oven.

"I did that all by myself," she said. "I got everything going." It was true. The Wishwells' modern kitchen was very busy doing nothing. Ebenezer rubbed his hands in glee.

"But that's not all," said Virginia. "Look what I found in the hall cupboard."

The Spooks looked at the rectangular object on wheels that Virginia pointed to. It had a long tube at one end and a wire at the other.

"What is it?" Hubert asked.

"It's a sucking and blowing machine. Watch." Virginia plugged the lead into the wall socket. Already quite at home with plugs and switches, she pressed a button on the machine. The motor started and the tube wriggled. Virginia pointed the tube at a tennis ball the twins had left under the hall table. The ball was sucked towards the machine and became glued to the nozzle.

"Now watch," said Virginia. She pressed another button. The machine blew air outwards and the ball flew across the hall. Then she switched the machine off.

"It's wonderful," said Hubert.

"Oh, it is!" said Ebenezer, for he had been forming a plan as he watched.

"Well done, Mistress Virginia! Well done, all of you! A very good night's work indeed.

And I have an idea that will get us off to an even better start. Help me get this machine upstairs and I'll show you what we must do."

As the first grey of dawn began to lighten the sky, an expectant stillness descended on the Grange. Soon it would be day and the Wishwells would awake. Soon they would know about hauntings.

6
The Ghost Hunters

Mr Wishwell spluttered into wakefulness. He opened his eyes and shut them again as he stretched. Pulling back the bed covers, he sat up. Unusually, the curtains were wide open and sunlight filled the bedroom. He looked in some surprise at the tissues which covered the floor and the end of the bed like giant snowflakes.

"What on earth has been going on here?" His face became stern. He nudged his wife. "Wake up, Sandra, and look at this." Mrs Wishwell opened her eyes.

"What time is it?" she asked. "Better not lie in too long. There's lots to do."

"Exactly. Hardly the time for practical jokes," said Mr Wishwell. "The twins can get in here and clear up at once."

"Oh, no!" said Mrs Wishwell, looking around the room.

"They *are* naughty." She heaved herself out of bed and began to pick up the tissues.

"Leave them, love," commanded Mr Wishwell. "The twins can pick them up." He put on his dressing gown.

On the landing Mr Wishwell stood listening expectantly. Strangely, there was no sound from the twins' bedrooms. He walked towards the bathroom. Being a little bleary-eyed, he didn't see the lead stretching under the bathroom door, nor did he notice Virginia poised by the socket, ready to switch on. He pushed open the door. Virginia pressed the switch and the blowing machine roared into action. The pink waves in the bath flew up and slapped into Mr Wishwell's face, perfectly directed by Mary and Hubert, who waved the blowing machine's nozzle triumphantly. Mr Wishwell let out an angry roar and charged along the landing, trailing festoons of toilet roll behind him, and tripping over the lead as he went.

"Wayne, Tracy," he bellowed. "Out here at once."

How he expected the twins to be operating

the machine and to be in their bedroom at the same time is hard to imagine.

Mrs Wishwell put her head out of the bedroom door.

"What's the matter now, Desmond?" she asked. Instead of a reply she heard outraged yells as Mr Wishwell marched the twins to

the bathroom. Mrs Wishwell followed and gasped when she saw the mess. Tracy and Wayne also stared in some surprise, especially at their father, who had a blob of shaving foam wobbling on the end of his nose.

"But we didn't do it," spluttered Wayne.

"No, of course we didn't," said Tracy.

The denial only seemed to redouble Mr Wishwell's fury.

"Don't lie to me!" he stormed.

"My new pink carpet," sobbed Mrs Wishwell. "Ruined." The twins were marched into their parents' bedroom.

"Now I suppose you're going to tell me you didn't do this either?" snarled Mr Wishwell. The twins looked at the scattered tissues.

"We didn't," they said.

"Well, if you didn't who did?" asked Mr Wishwell. Not waiting for a reply, he went on, "You can start clearing up at once. Go on, get on with it."

"But we didn't do it. We didn't! Why should we have to clear up when we didn't do it?" shouted Wayne.

"Of course you did it! There's no one else here to do it," yelled Mr Wishwell.

"We're not lying. We're not!" cried Tracy, furious at the injustice of it all. "You never ever believe us. We didn't do it."

Mr Wishwell went quiet.

"Clear these tissues up or else." His upper lip twitched ominously and the blob of shaving foam wobbled from his nose.

"Or else what?" said Tracy.

Mr Wishwell's eyes narrowed. "Or else you'll be sorry."

Tracy grabbed the box and began stuffing tissues into it. "You're never fair to us."

"Never, ever," said Wayne, setting to work.

"Not another word," said Mr Wishwell, in that same deadly tone of voice. He stood and watched them until a wail of dismay sent him hurrying downstairs.

"Now what?" said Tracy.

"Something else we're going to get the blame for, I suppose," said Wayne.

"I think we should run away from home," said Tracy. "That'd show them."

"Someone did this though," mused Wayne.

"You're right," Tracy said. "But who?"

It didn't take the twins long to stuff the tissues back in the box. When they had finished they went to the bathroom and began to pick up the pink toilet roll.

"Most of it we'll have to throw away because of the shaving foam," said Tracy.

"I suppose you think the baked bean tin a very funny surprise?" said Mr Wishwell, suddenly bursting into the bathroom.

"What baked bean tin?" asked Tracy.

"Don't pretend you don't know what I'm talking about. It doesn't cut any ice with me. The one you left on the living room floor," said Mr Wishwell. "And if I've told you once, I've told you a hundred times. You are not to touch the kitchen appliances."

Tracy and Wayne didn't even bother to say "We didn't." Instead, Tracy asked what was the matter with them.

"You know perfectly well," said Mr Wishwell. "All switched on."

Curiosity got the better of the twins then. A baked bean tin left on the living room floor, appliances turned on in the kitchen, tissues scattered, loo roll unrolled and shaving foam squirted everywhere . . . . Those were the sort of things they might have done, but for once hadn't.

"When you've finished clearing up go back to your rooms and stay there until further notice," said Mr Wishwell, leaving them to get on with it.

The twins had a room each. They were entered by separate doors on the landing. Once inside, however, you could move from room to room by a connecting door in the adjoining wall. Once the clearing up was done, Wayne joined Tracy in her room. The two of them sat on Tracy's bed and tried to solve the problem of the night's mysterious happenings.

"If you want to know what I think," said Wayne, "it was burglars. They were a bit hungry so they had some baked beans and then before they nicked anything they switched everything on to see if it worked. Then when they were ready to steal things Dad woke up, so they scarpered."

Tracy didn't think much of this theory. It

took her only a moment or two to demolish it.

"First thing, there's no sign of any break-in. Second, what would burglars want to waste their time throwing tissues and loo roll about for? No, it definitely wasn't burglars."

"Okay, know-all, what then?"

Tracy looked Wayne full in the eye and said, "I think it was ghosts."

Wayne leapt from the bed, dragging the

bed cover with him. He pulled it over his head and ran around the room flapping his arms so that the cover swirled and swayed.

"Whoo whoo whoo whoo," he wailed. "I am the ghost of the Grange and I've come to haunt you oo oo oo!"

"Shut up and listen," said Tracy, pulling the cover from Wayne's head. "If no one broke in – which they didn't – and we didn't do it – which we didn't – then it must have been ghosts."

"We could've done it sleep-walking," said Wayne.

Tracy looked at him dubiously. She hadn't thought of that, but it seemed unlikely, as neither of them had ever sleep-walked before.

"No." Tracy had made up her mind. "It's ghosts. I feel it in my bones."

"Well, if it's ghosts, you're going to have to prove it," said Wayne.

"All right," said Tracy. "I will."

"How?"

"By having a ghost hunt, that's how." Wayne's eyes lit up. A ghost hunt. He didn't think he believed in ghosts but he was very willing to try and find some.

When Mr Wishwell finally relented and told the twins they could come out they ran to the landing and slid down the banisters, eager for their breakfast. Mrs Wishwell, who was much more forgiving than her husband, never liked the twins to be confined for long. Besides, she knew from experience that they were always much worse once they were let out again. She was in the kitchen, anticipating wild behaviour, when they burst in. After breakfast, much to her surprise, the twins went to the living room and began quietly writing things in a notebook on the floor by the French windows.

Mr Wishwell looked approvingly at his offspring and felt his punishment had had the desired effect.

"Quite like normal children," he thought. If he had known the writing was called "A Manual for Ghost Hunters" by Tracy and Wayne Wishwell, he might not have felt so easy. But the twins had no intention of telling anyone what they were up to. The ghost hunt was a secret.

"The most important thing is to hunt in the middle of the night," said Tracy.

"How do you know?" asked Wayne.

Tracy didn't know for sure. It was a guess. "Anyway, all that tissue throwing and stuff must have happened when we were asleep. We've got to set a trap."

"I don't think you can catch a ghost," said Wayne. "They walk through walls and things."

"I know," said Tracy. "We must trick them into doing things so that we can see where they are." She wrote down "TRICKS" in her notebook and underneath, "ONE." Then she chewed the end of her pencil. It wasn't going to be as easy as she'd imagined. She couldn't think of a single trick.

"We could leave out a box of tissues," said Wayne.

"Good idea," said Tracy and wrote "TISSUES" beside the 'ONE'.

"You can't see ghosts, can you? That's the whole point. They're invisible," said Wayne.

"Not all ghosts," said Tracy. "Anyway,

we'll be able to hear them, I expect. In books you always get ghostly sounds, like galloping horses."

"We haven't heard any galloping horses since we've been here," said Wayne.

"It might be something else." Tracy was getting impatient. "How long is it till bedtime?"

"Hours," said Wayne. Tracy threw down the notebook. "We'll have to do something else until then." She sighed.

"Let's set up the computer and play 'INVADERS FROM LARG'," said Wayne.

It wasn't long before the most gruesome battle sounds were coming from Tracy's room, supplemented by the twins' bloodcurdling yells. In the kitchen Mrs Wishwell heard them with satisfaction.

"They seem to be settling in well," she said as she handed a pile of plates to her husband.

"If you mean the move doesn't seem to have dampened their spirits, I agree," he said, putting the plates in a cupboard.

The twins spent an energetic day playing and exploring. At bedtime they had a bath and once in bed, to their surprise, felt sleepy.

"Don't forget," Tracy called from her room. "Don't go to sleep. We're on red alert."

"I won't," said Wayne, trying not to yawn.

Mrs Wishwell tucked Tracy up first and kissed her good night. "Sleep tight, love," she said.

As soon as she was gone Tracy nipped out of bed and placed a large box of tissues in the middle of the floor. She got back into bed and tried hard to fight the growing heaviness in her eyelids.

"Night night, poppet," said Mrs Wishwell to Wayne.

"Night night," he murmured, losing the battle to stay awake.

Mrs Wishwell switched off the lights and tiptoed to the landing, gently closing the door behind her. The click of the door, which should have been a signal for wakefulness, had the opposite effect. The ghost hunters fell fast asleep.

It was early when Mr and Mrs Wishwell went to bed. There seemed to have been an endless amount of sorting out to do and they were both exhausted. Mrs Wishwell looked in on the twins and smiled happily, as if these two sleeping figures were the most angelic creatures in the world. Soon she and Mr Wishwell were tucked up in bed too. They gave each other a quick goodnight kiss and switched off the light. In a few minutes they were as lost in dreams, as were the twins, leaving the Grange quiet and undisturbed but for the hoot of a distant owl.

At a minute past midnight a shimmering form drifted into Tracy's bedroom and up to her bed. It made certain Tracy was asleep before it glided to the computer, which was on a table by the window. Hubert had found another television screen . . . .

There was a click as the computer was switched on. Hubert wanted to see if it had people in it like the box downstairs in the living room. He waited. But no men appeared, only some writing. He tried to read what it said. It looked like "Vulcan 84".

There was a whole tray of buttons with letters and numbers in front of the screen. He pressed some at random. Hubert was sure that if he pressed the right buttons moving pictures would appear. Buttons clicked as he tried again and again.

Click, click, click. The clicks made a pattern of sound that slowly wormed its way through Tracy's sleep until she awoke. She was aware at once of something unusual happening. Slowly she lifted her head and,

looking around her, found the room aglow with light from the computer screen. She knew the clicking came from the computer but no one was there. Tracy stared, her eyes wide like saucers. She felt a chill in the room and goose pimples on her arms.

"Yes," she thought. "That's how you recognize ghosts. By the coldness." She didn't move. She just watched. But try as she might, she could see nothing. The clicks stopped and the coldness seeped away. Tracy knew that whatever it was had gone, leaving the computer switched on. She swung herself out of her bed and tiptoed into Wayne's room. She shook him gently.

"Wayne, wake up," she said. "The ghosts have switched on the computer. Now's our chance."

7
Spooks in the Night

Tracy and Wayne tiptoed downstairs. Wayne was wondering whether Tracy was teasing him and had switched on the computer herself or whether someone, or something else really had done it. Tracy was earnest and tense as they crept across the hall. She gave the living room door a gentle push. It swung open. Glare from the television filled the room. Only the picture was on, no sound. And Wayne knew at once that they were on a real ghost hunt. Nothing was ever left on in their house; Mrs Wishwell saw to that. The television must have been switched on after their parents had gone to bed. There was a chill in the air that made the twins shiver. Tracy signalled a retreat.

The Spooks were left spellbound, watching a pirate movie made before the days of sound. Already they were in danger of becoming television addicts. After their early morning success, they seemed to have forgotten about haunting the Grange. They hadn't even noticed when Tracy and Wayne opened the living room door. The pirate battle that raged on the screen held their attention completely.

Upstairs the twins held a council of war.

"It's true," said Wayne. "You can't see them but somehow you can feel them." He rubbed his arms as if they were still chilled.

"That's a bit of a problem," said Tracy. "They can see us, but we can't see them. If we're going to scare them we're going to have to take them by surprise."

"*Should* we try to scare them?"

"Yes, we should. That'll pay them back for making all that mess we got the blame for."

"I expect it was meant to frighten us," said Wayne.

"Well, it didn't. I'm not scared. Are you?" said Tracy.

Wayne thought for a moment. "No, I'm not scared," he said.

"Good," said Tracy. "Let's think. What do

we know about them?"

"We know they like telly," said Wayne.

"Yes, and we know when they're about, it suddenly gets cold."

"Tracy," said Wayne. "Do you remember in the stables when we went up to the hayloft? It was cold then. And there was wind and a lot of cobwebs."

"So?"

"I reckon it was ghosts then. It might have been them that knocked us back. They might have saved us from falling down the hole."

"Do you think?" said Tracy. "Well, if we scare them now they might stop making such a mess of things all the time. We got told off rotten for the cobwebs."

"I can't think how to scare a ghost," said Wayne. "Unless . . .," and he had a brilliant idea. It popped into his head in a second, as all his best ideas did. "Trace, we can pretend to be ghosts!" he burst out.

"Shush," said Tracy, clapping her hand over Wayne's mouth. "Not so loud." Wayne pulled Tracy's hand away.

"We can dress up in sheets," he whispered.

"We can throw glitter over them," said Tracy.

"We can wave our football rattles," said Wayne.

"And whoop the whoopee cushion," said Tracy, really excited by the plan. "And I've got streamers in my desk drawer as well."

"We must howl and clank chains," said Wayne.

"We haven't got any chains," said Tracy. "But we could put lots of leggo in a pillowcase and clank that."

"Yeah," said Wayne. "Let's go." Tracy grabbed Wayne's hand in the dark.

"Don't rush," she said. "We must close your bedroom door and switch on the light. Do everything as quiet as mice."

Wayne padded softly to the door, shut it and switched on the light. Tracy helped Wayne pull the sheet from his bed. The pillow was pulled from the pillowcase. From the cupboard Tracy took a box. Wayne held the pillowcase while Tracy tipped the contents of the box into it. It was the leggo. Try as she might to do it quietly, the leggo clattered. The twins held their breath and waited, but nothing stirred.

Tracy tiptoed into her room, where the computer was still on. It gave her enough light to find the whoopee cushion and some streamers from amongst the jumble of things on the floor. She collected the glitter from her desk drawer, then unmade her bed, wrapped the sheet around her shoulders and went back to Wayne.

"If only the sheets were white!" she sighed. "Candy-green striped and candy-orange striped is all wrong. They'll know we're not ghosts."

"Not at first they won't," said Wayne. "The element of surprise will fool them. Where are the streamers?"

"Here," said Tracy, handing two over.

Wayne tied the pillowcase to a belt, which he secured around his waist. Tracy stuffed the whoopee cushion into the back of her pyjamas and put the remaining streamers in her pocket. She held the glitter ready in one hand and a football rattle in the other.

Wayne pulled his sheet over his head. He tucked a football rattle in his belt and carried the streamers. Duly armed, the twins set out.

"Be careful not to trip," said Tracy as she turned off the light.

"I will," whispered Wayne and he opened the door.

The twins felt their way to the top of the stairs, their eyes growing slowly accustomed to the dark. Laden as they were, they found it difficult to move quietly. The sheets rustled and every time the leggo bricks clattered Wayne froze. It took them several minutes to get downstairs.

When the twins arrived at the last step they breathed a sigh of relief. So far so good! At the living room door they paused. The credits for the pirate film were rolling down the screen. The Spooks were stirring, as if waking from some enchantment. With two bloodcurdling yells the twins charged.

The Spooks rose, startled and shimmering. Silver and red glitter floated about them and mingled with the two howling sheet-covered figures. The Spooks held their ground and took in the situation.

"Bah," exclaimed Ebenezer crossly. He hated being startled. Virginia grasped Mary's hand and ran with her to the safety of Mr Wishwell's bookcase, where they sat on the top shelf to watch. Football rattles were

drawn and the dreadful noise sent Ebenezer scurrying for the peace of the hall. Hubert sat on the television amidst all the commotion and grinned.

"Streamers," cried Tracy, shooting one skywards. It fell through Hubert and draped the television set.

"Oo oo oo oo," wailed the twins, throwing more streamers.

The room was a chaos of swirling sheets and deafening noise when, with a wicked smile, Hubert suddenly switched off the television. The room plunged into darkness. Unable to see, the twins tripped over their sheets. Wayne crashed into the sofa where the leggo bag was wrenched from his belt, scattering leggo across the floor. Tracy ran over it and cried out in pain as her bare feet were spiked by its sharp corners. She tripped and fell, sitting hard on the whoopee cushion. As its long moan died away, the light flashed on.

Mr Wishwell stood glowering in the doorway. The twins blinked in the sudden brightness. Tracy rubbed her feet. Wayne untangled himself from his sheet and tried to cover up the place where his foot had gone through it. Hubert glided to the book-case and watched with Virginia and Mary. Mr Wishwell, speechless, surveyed the mess.

"It's ghosts," said Tracy at last. She shivered. "They're still in here."

The Spooks shimmered and were gone.

"What nonsense," said Mr Wishwell. "I don't want to hear any excuses. I should have thought after the last fiasco you would have learnt your lesson. I see I was mistaken. Go straight back to bed. You can sort out this mess in the morning."

The twins trooped forlornly upstairs, dragging their sheets behind them. The Spooks watched from the landing banisters. Mary flicked the light on and off in sympathy. She felt sorry for the twins.

"You see," said Tracy. "Ghosts."

"Rubbish," said Mr Wishwell. "A fluctuation of current. It's the sort of thing that happens when you live in the country."

Mr Wishwell stood over the twins as they helped each other remake their beds. He made sure they were both tucked up before switching off the computer and the lights, then, with a curt goodnight, he went back to his own bed.

As soon as she was sure he was gone Tracy got out of bed and felt her way into Wayne's room.

"Wayne," she whispered. "You asleep?"

"No."

"They were on the landing."

"Never."

"They flashed the light."

"It wasn't ghosts. You heard what Dad said."

"He was wrong. His and Mum's door was open. The light was on in there. That didn't go off when the landing light did. I saw."

"Are you sure?" Wayne sat up. "We made a bit of a mess of that ghost hunt," he said.

"I know," said Tracy. "I forgot about the noise waking Mum and Dad. We're going to be in for it in the morning."

"That's why we've got to think of something now," said Wayne.

"Well, we know they like watching television. Why don't we set up a computer game for them. Something quiet."

"The chess game," said Wayne. "They might know how to play chess and it's great when you take a piece. The castle turns into a giant and splats things and the queen capows everything. It's only a tiny bit noisy."

"Yeah," said Tracy. "And Dad said it was an educational game. Remember?"

The twins crept to the computer and switched it on. The screen lit up and the words "Vulcan 84" appeared on the screen. Wayne spelt out "GAME space D" on the keyboard and the words came up on the screen. He pressed return. "LOAD FROM DISC" flashed on to the screen.

"Have you got the disc?" he asked.

"I'm looking for it," Tracy replied. "It's difficult seeing what's what in this light."

Goose pimples ran up her arms. She was too busy trying to find the chess disc to notice, but Wayne shivered.

"Trace," he whispered. "I think one of them's in here."

"Here it is." Tracy shivered too. "Yes, I see

what you mean."

Tracy loaded the disc into the machine and Wayne pressed return. There was a moment's whirring and "CHESS FOR EVERYONE" announced itself on the screen.

"Shall we show them how?" said Wayne.

"No," whispered Tracy. "Leave it like that. If anything's different by morning we'll know they had a go."

"Let's go back to bed then," said Wayne. He was cold and tired.

"Yes," said Tracy, her teeth chattering. "Let's."

Hubert grinned. He liked the twins. He waited until they were settled in bed and he could hear the sound of their sleepy breathing, then he drifted from the room and returned with the other Spooks. The four of them gathered around the computer screen.

"I don't see how you can play chess on one of these boxes," said Ebenezer. "The pieces will fall on the floor."

Hubert pushed the computer's joy stick and found it moved a small rectangle across the screen.

"I think that the stick and the blob are how it works," said Mary. "But you've got to press some of these buttons as well."

"You work it all out," said Virginia, languidly running her fingers through her ghostly tresses, "and when you have I'll come and play."

"It's all fiddlesticks, if you ask me," said Ebenezer. "I'm going back downstairs to see what's what." The others knew he really meant "see what's on television".

Mary and Hubert spent the rest of the night trying to work the computer. The best thing that happened was that they got a picture of a chessboard with all the pieces lined up ready for a game. They couldn't get it to play. It was frustrating. If only they knew what to do! They kept trying for hours but got nowhere. Hubert looked at Tracy. She was still fast asleep.

"Maybe the twins would teach us."

"How can we ask them?" said Mary.

"There must be a way," said Hubert. "I know." He picked up a stray crayon from the floor and with wobbly letters wrote on the mirror: "HOW DO YOU PLAY CHESS BY MACHINE?"

8
Hubert's Revenge

The twins woke late the next morning. When they finally stirred it was half past ten. Mr Wishwell had wanted to wake them at eight o'clock, but Mrs Wishwell had told him not to be so mean.

"Children will be children," she said. "We're lucky ours have got such well-developed imaginations. I'd never have thought of a ghost hunt when I was young." She smiled affectionately. Mr Wishwell went into a huff but on reflection Mrs Wishwell's words made him feel secretly proud of his twins.

"Not that they're getting off scot-free," he said to himself.

"Tracy," said Wayne when he pulled back the curtains. "Tracy." Wayne shook her awake. "Look at this." Tracy rubbed her eyes in an effort to make them see.

"Yes," she said blearily. "We left the computer on." Tracy's brain had not yet caught up with the events of last night.

"Yes, and this," said Wayne. "On the mirror. They've written a message."

Tracy's brain caught up with a jolt. She tumbled out of bed and read "HOW DO YOU PLAY CHESS BY MACHINE?"

"Cor," she said. "They've communicated."

"And look! They pressed the carriage return key as well. They set the chess game to start but got stuck."

Wayne's excitement was infectious.

"The ghosts are real," Tracy cried, dancing round the room. "The Grange is haunted! Hooray."

"We'd better get this crayon off the mirror," said Wayne. "Mum and Dad had better not see it. And don't forget we've got to clear up downstairs."

By the time the twins came down to breakfast their rooms were tidy, the computer was switched off and the mirror was spotlessly clean. They had washed, combed their hair and cleaned their teeth. They went straight

101

to the living room. Streamers lay draped over the furniture, leggo lay scattered and silver and red glitter sparkled on the carpet.

"Come on," said Tracy. "Let's get stuck in. "I'll get the vacuum cleaner." Wayne ran upstairs for the leggo box.

When the twins came back into the room something was different. Wayne put down the box. "What's been going on?"

"Someone's put all the streamers on the sofa!" said Tracy.

"Do you think it was them?" Wayne asked.

"Might have been Mum," said Tracy. But it wasn't Mrs Wishwell. She called to them from the kitchen, "Leave the living room until after breakfast." The twins walked backwards out of the room, hoping to see something move. Nothing did.

In the kitchen they sat at the table and ate their muesli without a word. Mrs Wishwell was pleased. There was usually such an argument about it. Mr Wishwell was suspicious. Good behaviour from the twins always made him uneasy.

"I'm glad to see you've good appetites," he

said, as the twins began tucking into their boiled eggs. They restrained themselves from splatting the eggshells and, when they had finished, asked politely if they could return to tidying the living room. Mrs Wishwell beamed at them.

"Before you go," said Mr Wishwell, "listen to me. When you've finished you are to stay in your rooms until lunch time. And there is to be no computer games for a week."

"Dad!" exclaimed Wayne. Tracy kicked him under the table and looked innocently at her father. Wayne didn't protest again.

"I'll leave the word processing disc."

"And the chess?" asked Wayne.

"Certainly not. I suggest you write lots of stories. A ghost story might be appropriate under the circumstances."

Tracy looked at him suspiciously wondering what he meant. Mr Wishwell didn't seem to mean anything much. The next thing he did was order them back to the living room.

"Poor dears," said Mrs Wishwell. "I think you're too hard on them." That wasn't how she felt when she went upstairs and took the sheets off the twins' beds for washing. She was furious when she saw the rip where Wayne's foot had gone through.

"Oh," she exclaimed. "And that's a new sheet too!"

Nothing else had changed when the twins went back into the living room. They carried the streamers to the kitchen and piled them in the bin. Wayne picked up the leggo and plumped up the cushions while Tracy vacuumed the carpet. By the time they had finished, the room was as neat and tidy as it had ever been. They looked out of the window. It was a lovely sunny day and a slight breeze ruffled the leaves on the wisteria as if inviting them outside. But it was no good. They trooped upstairs to their rooms and found that their father had already collected the computer discs.

"No computer games means it's going to be a really boring morning," said Tracy with a sigh. "I suppose we'll have to read or something."

Wayne liked reading, unlike Tracy, who liked to be active all the time. He was quite happy to continue reading his space monster book. In fact, he was eager to know what happened next and settled quietly with the book on his knee.

Tracy paced her room and then she paced Wayne's. She did quite a lot of gloomy walking up and down before her face suddenly lit up and she rushed to the computer to switch it on. Then she began to rummage amongst a pile of bits and pieces in a box. With a triumphant cry she pulled out a computer disc and put it in the computer. She pressed carriage return. The machine whirred and the words "EASY WORD" appeared on the screen.

"What are you going to do? Write a story?" asked Wayne. He thought it unlikely, but you never could tell with Tracy.

"Nope," said Tracy. "I'm going to ask a question and see if we can get an answer."

She pressed option one and when the computer asked for the filename she typed in "SPOOKS".

"Why spooks?" asked Wayne.

"I don't know," said Tracy. She shivered.

"My fingers sort of went that way." The screen was blank. She typed onto it "SORRY WE CAN'T PLAY CHESS BY MACHINE. DAD HAS TAKEN THE DISC. WHO ARE YOU? TYPE IN YOUR ANSWER BY PRESSING THE LETTERS ON THE KEYBOARD. THANK YOU. LOVE TRACY."

Tracy sat back and waited. After what seemed like an age the room chilled and she sat up expectantly.

"Wayne! Watch!" She whispered.

There was a click on the keyboard and a letter W appeared on the screen underneath Tracy's message. The W was followed by an E and a whole string of other letters.

"WEWILLGETYOURDAD.

WEARETHESPOOKS."

"What's it say?" asked Wayne, puzzled.

"I'm not sure," said Tracy. "Oh, I get it. They don't know about the space bar for making spaces between letters."

"Quick. Work it out," said Wayne.

"We will get your dad. We are the Spooks!" said Tracy. "Oh, heck. They're going to haunt Dad."

"I think they're cross about not being able to play chess by machine," said Wayne.

"We *are*," said Hubert and Mary melting through the wall. On the way downstairs they drifted past Ebenezer.

"Where are you going, Master Hubert, Mistress Mary?" he asked.

"Outside," said Mary. "To play," she added as an afterthought. Ebenezer looked at them suspiciously.

"I don't want you getting up to mischief," he said.

"As if we would, Ebenezer," Mary said, looking him full in the eye. Ebenezer was not convinced.

They found Mr Wishwell in the old stables loading up a wheelbarrow with a fork and spade. He went to look for his gardening gloves and as soon as he was gone Mary lifted out the spade and Hubert the fork. They leaned them against the wall. When Mr Wishwell came back with his gloves he stared at the empty wheelbarrow. He scratched his head and put the tools back in the barrow, then wheeled it out of the stableyard to the door which led into the old kitchen garden. This was surrounded by a high wall, its red bricks crumbling with age and neglect. Mr Wishwell proposed to restore the garden himself. He was going to dig it, manure it and plant seeds for the spring.

He turned the handle of the door and pushed, but for some reason the door would not budge. He pushed harder. He had no idea, of course, that Mary and Hubert were on the other side, pushing to keep it closed. In one last desperate attempt Mr Wishwell heaved himself at the door with all his weight. Mary and Hubert stopped pushing. Mr Wishwell catapulted through the door and nose-dived into a bed of stinging nettles.

Mary and Hubert were delighted. They danced about him, feeling he was truly rewarded for his bad temper – which this event did nothing to improve. He rubbed dock leaves into his stings and studied the door. There was no apparent reason he could see for it to stick.

Mr Wishwell let out an angry grunt and wheeled his tools to the patch he was going

to dig. He had set himself the task of digging one long row. It was hot, hard work and took him much longer than he had thought it would. The weeds he threw into the barrow kept falling out and little midges bit him all over, yet when he looked for these biting insects they were nowhere to be seen.

He had no idea that it was Mary and

Hubert who were pinching him and dropping his weeds. When he finally reached the end of the row and looked at his watch it was two o'clock.

"Oh, heavens," he said. "I've forgotten to let the twins out."

The twins were longing to leave their rooms but didn't dare without their father's permission.

"We'll die of starvation if he doesn't come soon," moaned Tracy. "Maybe they scared him so much he's run away."

"And where's Mum?" said Wayne.

"She's gone shopping," said Tracy, glumly.

Mrs Wishwell had driven off earlier in the Wishwells' green car. She should have been back by now, but she had taken Virginia as an invisible passenger. Virginia had never been in a car before and it turned out to be a fraught expedition for Mrs Wishwell. Virginia wanted to help drive and switched off the engine several times at the most inconvenient moments. She wobbled the steering wheel the wrong way and played with the handbrake while the car was moving. The car lurched and bumped and swerved and stalled. Mrs Wishwell's nerves were in tatters when, at last, they arrived at the big supermarket.

Her problems didn't stop there. Virginia wanted plenty of time to gaze at the shelves and kept turning Mrs Wishwell's trolley in the direction she wanted to look. It ran over Mrs Wishwell's toes on several occasions. There was only one major mishap, however. This was when Virginia selected a tin of baked beans for Ebenezer, so that he would always be able to strike the witching hour.

Not being a very practical Spook, she took it from the bottom of the pile, causing the whole lot to crash across the supermarket floor. Virginia wasn't bothered, but Mrs Wishwell was. She nearly jumped out of her skin. Meanwhile, the trolley quickly filled with all sorts of things that Mrs Wishwell hadn't put in it.

At the checkout Mrs Wishwell was shocked by the size of her bill and the pile of goods she knew she hadn't selected – like the Mud Pack For Facial Beauty, the four different bottles of nail varnish and the six different bottles of fruit shampoo. She hated fruit shampoo. But it was too late to put it back. It had all been rung up on the till and she didn't want to make a fuss.

"It's been absolutely fascinating," said Virginia, as she watched Mrs Wishwell pile the boot with bag after bag of shopping, before gracefully reclining on the back seat and combing out her ghostly tresses with a sigh.

By the time Mrs Wishwell turned the car into the drive at the Grange she was quite exhausted. So was Virginia, but she was stretched languidly across the back seat, half asleep. It was two fifteen. The precise moment that Mr Wishwell opened Wayne's bedroom door and said to the twins, "You can come out now."

"Oh, Dad!" said Tracy. "We're half starved!"

Overcome by a sense of guilt, Mr Wishwell ushered the twins downstairs and into the kitchen and gave them each a bag of crisps.

"To keep you going," he said. Then he hurried out to help Mrs Wishwell unload the shopping from the car.

As the twins began unpacking one of the shopping bags in the kitchen, the familiar chill invaded the room as Mary and Hubert began to help too. If you can call it that. Soon shopping was all over the floor and the twins were thoroughly confused.

"What's happening?" asked Wayne.

"I think they're helping," said Tracy.

"Or not helping," said Wayne. "They're making a mess, and you know who's going to get the blame." A bag of sugar floated into the air.

"Cor," said Wayne. "Look at that!"

"Please, don't help any more," said Tracy to the bag of sugar. It fell to the floor and burst. Sugar spilled everywhere.

"Quick," said Tracy. "Dustpan." But it was too late. Mr and Mrs Wishwell came in with the last two bags of shopping.

"Sorry, Mum," said Tracy. "I'm really sorry. It was an accident."

The strain of the day told on Mrs Wishwell, looking round now at shopping spread here, there and everywhere and sugar all over the floor.

"This is the last straw," she cried. "Everything that could do, has gone wrong from the moment I set off down the drive. It was bad enough when I skidded at the traffic lights and found the handbrake on. And then the baked bean tins collapsed everywhere. But this, this is the last straw!"

Hubert hugged himself with delight. He had had sweet revenge for not being able to play chess by machine.

"If this is how you're going to behave you'll have to go to one of those holiday camps for the rest of the summer holidays," Mrs Wishwell snapped. "I can't take any more." She burst into tears.

"Mum," said Tracy in dismay. "We'll sort it out in no time."

"We were only trying to help," said Wayne and took his mother's hand.

"There, there, dear," said Mr Wishwell patting her on the back. "There's no need to cry." He looked pretty near to crying himself. The nettle stings on his face were bright pink.

Hubert's face fell and Mary looked aghast. Send the twins away! This was not what was supposed to happen.

Tracy and Wayne rushed to sweep up the sugar.

"What I want to know is," said Tracy between clenched teeth, "is it peace or war? It's all very well having ghosts but if they're going to make this sort of mess and keep getting us into trouble it's no fun at all."

9
Truce

Once again the twins found themselves confined upstairs.

"It's really not fair," complained Tracy. "We've spent ages in our rooms and we've been trying to be good."

"The Spooks are to blame," said Wayne.

Ebenezer, who was passing through, paused to listen when he heard the word Spooks.

"I wish they would flippin' well stop it," said Tracy. "And leave us alone."

"If they go on like this we'll get sent to the holiday camp," said Wayne, gloomily.

"Stop what?" wondered Ebenezer. He faded through the wall. In the living room he found Mr and Mrs Wishwell sitting exhausted on the sofa, discussing the twins behaviour.

"They're getting out of hand," said Mr

Wishwell. "Neither of us can control them." This was true, but the twins always knew how far they could go before disturbing the peace. Mary and Hubert Spook did not.

"They've never behaved this badly before," sighed Mrs Wishwell. "Do you think it's something to do with living in this house?" She shivered. "Goodness, it's cold in here."

"I shouldn't think so," said Mr Wishwell. "But you're right, their behaviour got worse after we moved in."

"Perhaps we should sell up and move," said Mrs Wishwell. Ebenezer gave a start of surprise. "I thought this was a dream house but if the twins are going to behave like this I'd rather move back to the estate."

"I don't think we should think about moving just yet," said Mr Wishwell. "We've only been here a few days. No, we must give them one more chance before we take any major decisions. If they don't improve we'll try sending them away to camp."

"I don't really want to send them away," said Mrs Wishwell.

"I know you don't, dear, but what else can we do?"

"Bah," said Ebenezer. "Something's been happening that I don't know about." He melted away.

Ebenezer assembled the Spooks in the attic amongst the smart new roof beams. Virginia draped herself against the large, black water tank and arranged her ghostly tresses neatly around her shoulders. Hubert and Mary sat hugging their knees. Ebenezer perched on a beam and said icily, "Mrs Wishwell is talking of leaving."

Virginia looked surprised. "Leaving the Grange?" She'd been so careful not to give the wrong impression when she went shopping. She hadn't done anything too startling. At least she couldn't *think* of anything. Nothing to make Mrs Wishwell imagine she was being haunted.

"Oh, dear," said Virginia. "I hope it's nothing to do with me."

"Why should it be?" inquired Ebenezer.

"I went shopping with Mrs Wishwell today. But I didn't do anything to frighten her. I'm sure I didn't."

"No, no, Mistress Virginia," said Ebenezer. "It was nothing to do with shopping. It was to do with the twins."

Hubert and Mary were looking hard at their knees and feeling uncomfortable.

"That leaves Mistress Mary and Master Hubert," said Ebenezer, turning his hollow gaze upon them. "What have you to say on the matter?"

Mary wriggled self-consciously. Hubert gave a little cough.

"Well . . ." they both said together.

"Yes?" said Ebenezer.

"Well," said Mary. "Hubert wanted to play chess by machine." Ebenezer nodded. "He couldn't make it work so he wrote a message on the mirror asking how to do it."

"Weren't the twins scared?" asked Virginia.

"Not a bit," said Mary. "They'd already guessed we were here."

"What happened was that after our hauntings and their hauntings the twins got all the blame. To punish them Mr Wishwell took away the bits that make the chess by machine work," said Hubert.

"So Hubert got angry," said Mary. "And so did I. I so wanted to play chess."

"What did you do?" asked Virginia.

"We haunted Mr Wishwell in the kitchen garden," said Mary.

"And broke a bag of sugar in the kitchen," said Hubert.

Ebenezer looked thoughtful.

"If the Wishwells do leave, in all probability no one else will come and live in the Grange," said Ebenezer. "It's true I started the hauntings. I wanted to scare the Wishwells. I see now it was a mistake."

"I think so too," said Virginia.

"Besides," said Ebenezer, "it's much more interesting now they're here." Virginia knew Ebenezer meant interesting because of the television. Already both she and Ebenezer made sure they didn't miss the serial "Happy Families". They sat down each day with Mr and Mrs Wishwell to watch it.

"How shall we stop them?" asked Mary.

"We really like the twins, and I know they'll teach us chess by machine when Mr Wishwell gives them the special bits back," said Hubert.

"We must help restore the twins to their parents' good books. That's what we must do," said Ebenezer. "We must think of a way quickly. There's no time to be lost."

Unfortunately for the Spooks, however, the twins were already plotting their revenge. They were cross and fed up.

"I want to teach the Spooks a lesson they won't forget," said Tracy. "If we're going to be bored, then so are they."

"That's it," said Wayne. "The television! Get them where it hurts."

"The television!" repeated Tracy. "Yes, we must fix it so they can't watch all-night films."

"Or play with the computer," said Wayne. "You know what we must do?"

Tracy's eyes glinted. "Switch off the electricity," she said. "We'll do it last thing tonight when Mum and Dad have gone to bed."

The Spooks meanwhile, were making plans of their own. Virginia was making a list of all the nice things the twins could do to please their parents – like bring them early morning tea in bed. They could lay the table for breakfast. They could tidy their rooms and, most especially, put away the things which still lay in piles on the floor from the first day they had moved in. And how pleased Mr Wishwell would be if one of the twins wrote a story!

"That's all very well, Mistress Virginia. But how are we going to get the twins to perform these wonderful deeds?" hissed Ebenezer.

"Easy. We do it ourselves," said Virginia.

"You *are* clever, Virginia," said Mary. "I wish I'd thought of that."

"It'll be just as before, when they got the blame," said Hubert. "Only this time they'll get a pat on the back instead."

"And won't be sent away," said Mary.

"We hope," added Ebenezer. "We'll meet after the Wishwells have gone to bed to carry out our plan."

The rest of the day was unusually peaceful. The twins were as good as gold. They kept a special look-out for Spooks but saw nothing suspicious.

By the time Mrs Wishwell kissed the twins good night, all the naughty things they had done seemed no more than a bad dream. This was what she told Mr Wishwell when she went downstairs and found him dozing on the sofa in front of the television. She sank down next to him, obliging Ebenezer to move in order to see the screen.

"I'll go up and say good night to them," said Mr Wishwell, smiling. When he reached the landing he popped his head round Tracy's door. Tracy was propped up on her pillow reading. Mr Wishwell crossed to her bed and gave her a bearhug, thereby causing her to lose her place in the book. She didn't protest. She smiled and kissed her father on the cheek. She knew reading impressed him.

"Night night, Dad," she said.

"Don't read too late now, will you love?" said Mr Wishwell.

"I won't," said Tracy.

"Goodnight, Wayne," said Mr Wishwell, sitting down on his son's bed. He ruffled Wayne's hair and gave him a hug and a kiss.

"Don't you read too late, will you, Wayne?"

"I won't, Dad," said Wayne. "But it's difficult to stop. It's such a good book."

"What is it?"

"Monsters from Space. It's creepy."

"Sounds it," said Mr Wishwell, getting up. "See you in the morning."

At ten thirty, when the news was over, the Wishwells switched off the television. Ebenezer sighed. He had hoped to watch a little longer.

"Leave the coffee cups 'til the morning," said Mrs Wishwell with a yawn. "Let's go straight to bed."

"We'll see to them," hissed Ebenezer. But, of course, the Wishwells didn't hear him. They switched off the lights and went wearily upstairs.

When Tracy was sure her parents had closed their bedroom door for the last time she got out of bed, tied her dressing gown tight and fumbled for her slippers. She tiptoed into Wayne's room.

"Wake up, Wayne," she said, and shook him. Wayne grunted. "We've got to turn the electricity off, remember?"

"All right, all right," said Wayne. "I'm awake." Tracy pulled the duvet off him.

"Get up," she ordered.

"Couldn't we switch the electricity off tomorrow night?" Wayne asked. "It's freezing."

"No, we can't. We're going to do it now. We're going to show those Spooks a thing or two," said Tracy. "Get up."

"Bah," said Ebenezer, who was eavesdropping just inside the door. "Just as well I checked on them. Behave like little angels when they're planning mischief!" He slipped the key from Wayne's door and melted through the wall. He locked the door from

the outside without so much as a sound and quickly moved along the landing to Tracy's door, where he did the same. He took the precaution of placing both keys in the vase Mrs Wishwell had put as decoration on the landing window sill.

Downstairs in the kitchen the Spooks gathered in readiness for their night's work. Ebenezer told them he had locked the twins' bedroom doors.

"They were on their way to switch off the electricity," he said. "To stop us watching television, no less! Master Hubert, Mistress Mary, you must talk to them. We want a truce, not out-and-out war."

"Yes, off you go, you two. We'll tidy up downstairs and get things ready for the morning," said Virginia with a toss of her ghostly head.

Mary and Hubert sped upstairs and found Tracy seething with frustration by her bedroom door.

"Well if they're locked, they're locked," said Wayne. "Both keys are missing, so someone's done it on purpose."

"Yes, and I bet I know who!"

"Dad?"

"No, not Dad. The Spooks. How many of them are there? We don't even know that. There could be a whole army of them, for all we know," said Tracy. "Well, we can't do the electricity tonight, that's for sure."

"We could write them a rude message on the computer instead," said Wayne.

"Good idea," said Tracy.

Mary nudged Hubert. "Don't forget to look carefully to see how they do it," she said.

Tracy switched on the computer and fed in the Easy Word disc. She pressed carriage return and the machine whirred into action. "EASY WORD" appeared on the screen. She pressed option one and typed in "SPOOKS".

"Did you save the other messages?" asked Wayne.

"Nope. Forgot," said Tracy. The screen was blank. "What shall we say?"

Before the twins had time to think, the keyboard clicked and letters began to appear on the screen. The twins jumped back in surprise as "TRUCEPLEASE. WEARE-SORRY." appeared on the screen.

"Truce please. We are sorry," said Tracy.

"They want a truce," said Wayne. "Are they sorry they dropped the sugar bag?" The keyboard clicked. "YESWEARE."

"Well, that's something," said Wayne.

"Shall we have a truce?" Tracy asked.

"I think we should. I don't want to get sent away," said Wayne.

"Neither do I," said Tracy.

"Is it truce then?"

"It's truce," said Tracy.

Wayne bumped the carriage return key twice and typed "TRUCE space AGREED". Something invisible typed "HOORAY."

10
Peace at Last

Downstairs in the kitchen, Virginia and Ebenezer put the finishing touches to their plan. The living room had been tidied, the cushions on the sofa plumped and pummelled, and the dirty coffee cups placed in the washing-up machine. And the kitchen gleamed after Ebenezer had given everything a vigorous polish. Both Spooks were well pleased with their efforts.

"Time to go upstairs and see if it's peace at last," said Ebenezer.

They found Mary and Hubert deep in computer conversation with the twins.

"So, how many of you spooks are there?" Wayne asked. Hubert typed "FOUR". Mary wrote "MARY HUBERT VIRGINIA AND EBENEZER".

Tracy sparkled with excitement.

"Where do you come from?" she asked.

131

"FROM THE GRANGE. WE ALL LIVED HERE AND DIED HERE TRAGICALLY. ONCE WE WERE A HAPPY FAMILY. VIRGINIA, OUR OLDER SISTER, DIED FROM A BROKEN HEART. THEN I DIED FROM SCARLET FEVER. HUBERT DIED NEXT FROM A BROKEN NECK," came the reply.

"Let me tell what happened," said Hubert, and typed, "I FELL OFF MY PONY." He wasn't very proud of the fact but thought he'd better tell it anyway.

"EBENEZER WAS OUR BUTLER," he went on. "HE DIED TOO. A BARREL FELL ON HIS HEAD. OUR PARENTS WERE SAD WHEN WE WERE DEAD. WE TRIED TO TELL THEM WE WERE STILL HERE, BUT THEY GOT FRIGHTENED. THEY MOVED AWAY AND LEFT US THE GRANGE. WE MISSED THEM WHEN THEY WENT. THEN WE GOT USED TO BEING ON OUR OWN. OTHER PEOPLE CAME AND WE HAUNTED THEM. THEY WENT AWAY. BUT NOW YOU ARE HERE AND WE LIKE IT."

"When did you live here?" Tracy asked.

"A LONG TIME AGO, BEFORE CARS AND TELEVISIONS AND ELECTRIC MACHINES. WE HAD HORSES AND CARRIAGES."

Virginia smiled and Ebenezer faded onto the landing to collect the keys from the vase and unlock the bedroom doors.

"I don't think we'll be having any more problems with the twins," he mused. "I think we're friends now. Most satisfactory," he said, gliding back into Tracy's bedroom.

"Tell them it's time for bed. They don't want to get into any more trouble," said Ebenezer. Mary and Hubert sighed, but they knew Ebenezer was right.

"EBENEZER SAYS IT'S TIME FOR YOU TO GO TO BED," they wrote. "SLEEP TIGHT. GOOD NIGHT FROM THE SPOOKS."

"Good night," said Wayne. He asked the computer to save what the Spooks had written, so they could read it again in the morning.

"Please watch television as much as you

like," said Tracy. "And tomorrow we'll show you how to work the video."

"Good idea," said Wayne. "We've got lots of films on tape."

"The video," repeated Ebenezer. "What on earth is that?"

"You'll find out tomorrow, I expect," said Virginia and with a deep sigh she faded from the room.

"Thinking of her lost love again," said Mary.

"You can always tell when she is," said Hubert. "She gets that soppy look." The Spooks faded away and the twins switched off the computer.

"They sound nice for ghosts," said Tracy. "Don't you think?"

"I wish we could see them," said Wayne.

"Yes, I don't suppose we ever shall," said Tracy. "Do you think they wear old-fashioned clothes?"

"We'll have to ask them," Wayne yawned. Tiredness came creeping over him. "See you in the morning, Trace."

The twins fell asleep as soon as their heads

touched the pillow. The Spooks spent the night in the living room. They watched a whole film on television and when Hubert discovered a pack of cards they played whist. Then, towards dawn, Virginia asked Hubert to show her how to work the computer. He brought the Spooks file onto the screen, and underneath what was already written Virginia slowly typed "A GHOSTLY STORY".

"What are you writing a story for?" asked Hubert.

"To impress Mr Wishwell," said Virginia. "I've been thinking it up all night."

Hubert looked over Virginia's shoulder while she typed and read, "ONCE, MANY YEARS AGO, IN THIS OLD HOUSE, THE GRANGE, LIVED A LARGE AND HAPPY FAMILY. THERE WAS A MOTHER AND FATHER, AND THERE WERE TWELVE CHILDREN, FOUR BROTHERS AND EIGHT SISTERS. ALSO A BUTLER, A HOUSEKEEPER AND THREE MAIDS, A MANSERVANT, A GARDENER AND THREE GROOMS. THE ELDEST DAUGHTER WAS

BEAUTIFUL. SHE LOVED SIR ROLAND EARLANDER'S YOUNGEST SON, PEREGRINE, A LIEUTENANT IN THE KING'S FUSILIERS. IMAGINE HER DISTRESS WHEN SHE HEARD HER LOVE LAY SLAIN ON THE BATTLE-FIELD! THERE WAS NO CONSOLING HER. SHE PINED AWAY AND DIED OF LOVE. THE FAMILY WAS SAD WHEN SHE DIED. SHE WAS BURIED IN THE CHURCHYARD. HER BROTHERS AND SISTERS COVERED HER GRAVE WITH FLOWERS. AND EVEN TO THIS DAY SHE RETURNS TO THE OLD HOUSE, CALLING FOR HER LOST LOVE. THE END."

"There," said Virginia. "I think Mr Wishwell should be pleased with that, don't you?" Hubert grinned. "Yes, I suppose so," he said. He saved the story and switched off the computer.

"What's so funny?" asked Virginia.

"Nothing," said Hubert.

"Right," said Virginia, "you can help me tidy up these bedrooms."

The twins slept on undisturbed whilst the Spooks busied themselves with the tidying.

In the morning Mr and Mrs Wishwell awoke to find a steaming cup of tea waiting for each of them on the bedside table.

"Aren't they sweet?" said Mrs Wishwell, smiling happily. Mr Wishwell couldn't think who she meant for a moment. Then he realized she must be speaking of the twins. He felt sceptical. The twins bringing them tea in bed? It didn't seem very likely. Yet here was the tea, and suddenly he was filled with an overwhelming sense of optimism.

Perhaps they had turned over a new leaf.

More surprises were in store for them when they went downstairs. The breakfast was laid, the kitchen was spotless and the living room tidy.

"Oh, the dears," cried Mrs Wishwell in ecstasy. "What a wonderful surprise!"

When the twins came into the kitchen bleary-eyed from their late night they were met by Mr and Mrs Wishwell beaming a welcome and glowing with parental pride. The twins smiled sheepishly, glad to be in their parents' good books, but wondering what they had done to cause such pleasure. When they were thanked for the tea in bed they exchanged knowing looks. What other good things were they supposed to have done? They soon found out, for Mrs Wishwell chatted about nothing else all through breakfast.

After breakfast the twins hurried upstairs and drew back their curtains.

"Hey, Tracy," called Wayne. "There's something different in here."

"In here too," said Tracy, pulling open

her cupboard door to find all her possessions packed neatly away on the shelves. "My room's been tidied."

"So has mine."

"The Spooks really are on our side," she said.

Wayne switched on the computer. "I'm going to say thank you," he said, grateful not to have to do the tidying himself, since it was the one thing he hated.

The computer whirred and on to the screen flashed the words "A GHOSTLY STORY".

"Hey Tracy, look at this," said Wayne. "They've written something."

"It's brilliant," said Tracy as she read it. "Let's plug in the printer and make a copy." Wayne found the printer on the bottom shelf of Tracy's cupboard. Tracy loaded some paper and they set the printer going. In no time at all a copy of the story had been printed onto a piece of pink paper.

"I bet Virginia wrote that," said Tracy, running her eyes over the story once again. A head poked around the door.

"Hello, Dad," said Wayne.

"Goodness, you have been busy," said Mr Wishwell. "Everything's nice and tidy. What's that, Tracy?"

"A sort of story." Tracy blushed. She didn't want her father to read it. She knew he'd think she'd written it.

"Can I see?"

Reluctantly Tracy handed over the piece of pink paper.

Mr Wishwell read the story and smiled.

"My, my," he said. "Very nice. Very nice indeed. I'm glad there aren't real ghosts at the Grange though, aren't you?"

The twins didn't reply. Tracy put her hand out for the story.

"I'll let you have it back in a minute," said Mr Wishwell. "I'm sure your mother would like to read it."

Virginia followed Mr Wishwell and the piece of pink paper into the kitchen. She was extremely gratified that Mr Wishwell liked the story so much.

Mrs Wishwell read it and decided at once that Tracy was going to be a novelist when she grew up.

"Yes," sighed Virginia. "Everything is going according to plan."

Yet by the end of the morning the twins were finding being good, being polite and being tidy rather a strain.

Tracy had a large white wall in her room which she felt needed something big on it. "I could paint a picture," she said. "A giant mural."

"Better ask," said Wayne.

Tracy sighed. She knew what the answer would be and thought she'd do it anyway. She fetched her powder paints and put one hand on the tin of yellow paint. A voice at the back of her mind said "children's holiday camp", and her hand came off the tin as if it had been burnt.

"Let's go outside," said Tracy, wanting to take herself away from temptation.

For the rest of the day she and Wayne played outside. They climbed trees and explored the kitchen garden. They even helped their father with the weeding for a bit.

At teatime everyone gathered in the kitchen, Spooks and all. At last, Tracy dared to mention the children's holiday camp.

"Are you really going to send us to the children's camp?" she asked.

"No, you've both turned over a new leaf, we can see that and we're really pleased," said Mr Wishwell. "As a matter of fact, your mum and I were thinking we could all take a little holiday now we're settled in here. Before you start school and we start work again."

"Oh great, Dad, where?" asked Wayne.

"We thought Hunstey-on-Sea might be nice! What do you say?" smiled Mrs Wishwell.

The Spooks looked at one another as only Spooks can. None of them had ever seen the sea.

"Yes, that would be nice," the twins agreed.

"Just the four of us. There'll be lots for you children to do."

"Oh Mum," said Tracy, "it sounds great."

"And perhaps we can come too," hissed

Ebenezer. But, of course, the Wishwells didn't hear him.

"Yes," said Mrs Wishwell. "A quiet little family holiday. Nothing could be nicer. It'll mark the beginning of our living happily ever after in the Grange."

"Yes," said Mr Wishwell. "For that is what we shall do."

The twins smiled happily. So did the Spooks. For everything had turned out very well, considering.